To
Lily,

MERRY
CHRISTMAS

Love from,

....

'Twas the night before Christmas,
when all through the house,
Not a creature was stirring,
not even a mouse;

Lily's stocking was hung
by the chimney with care,
In hope that St. Nicholas
soon would be there.

Lily was nestled all snug in her bed,
While visions of candy canes danced in her head.
And Mom in her kerchief, and Dad in his cap,
Had just settled down for a long winter's nap.

When out on the street
there arose such a clatter,
Lily sprang from her bed
to see what was the matter.

The moon on the blanket
of new-fallen snow,
Shone bright as midday
on the objects below—

When, what to Lily's
wondering eyes should appear,
But a miniature sleigh
and eight tiny reindeer.

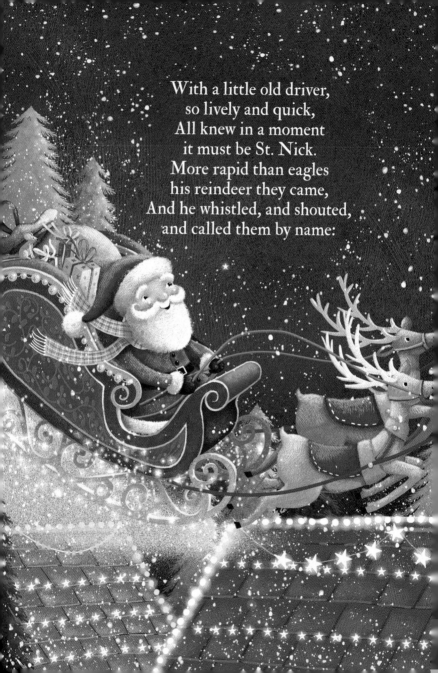

With a little old driver,
so lively and quick,
All knew in a moment
it must be St. Nick.
More rapid than eagles
his reindeer they came,
And he whistled, and shouted,
and called them by name:

"Now, Dasher! Now, Dancer!
Now, Prancer and Vixen!
On, Comet! On, Cupid!
On, Donder and Blitzen!
Take me to Lily's chimney;
follow my call!
Now dash away, dash away,
dash away all!"

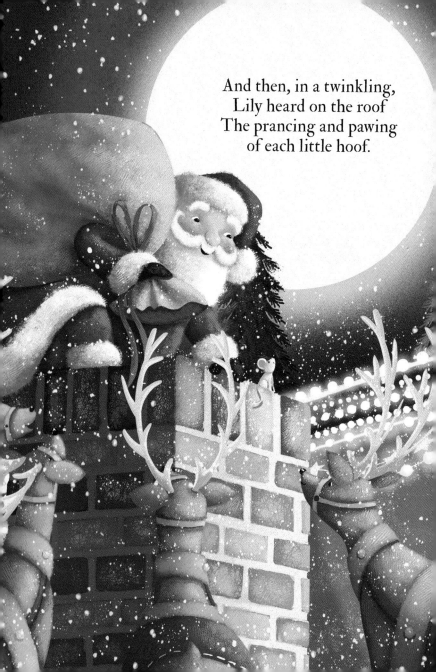

And then, in a twinkling,
Lily heard on the roof
The prancing and pawing
of each little hoof.

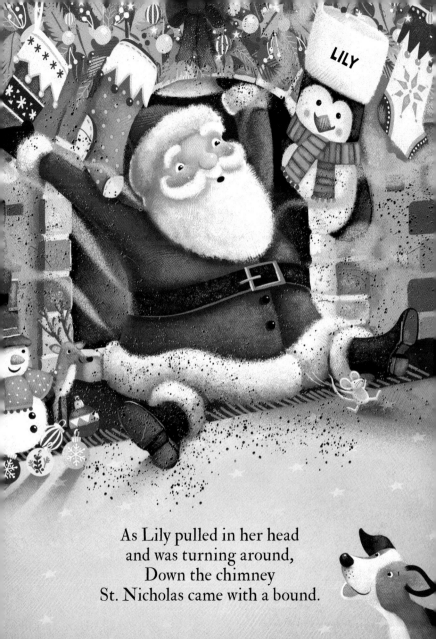

As Lily pulled in her head
and was turning around,
Down the chimney
St. Nicholas came with a bound.

He was dressed all in fur,
from his head to his foot,
And his clothes were all tarnished
with ashes and soot.
A bundle of toys he had
flung on his back,
And he looked like a peddler
holding his pack.

BLESS
OUR
HOME

His eyes–how they twinkled!
His dimples–how merry!
His cheeks were like roses,
his nose like a cherry.
His droll little mouth
was drawn up like a bow,
And the beard on his chin was
as white as the snow.

Dear Santa,
    Welcome to
my house!
I hope you enjoy the
yummy treats I have
left out for you.
    Love from your
    biggest fan,

Lily
xxx

A big sack of toys
he held tight in his fist,
And he glanced to see Lily
on top of his list.

SANTA'S
nice
list

To
Lily

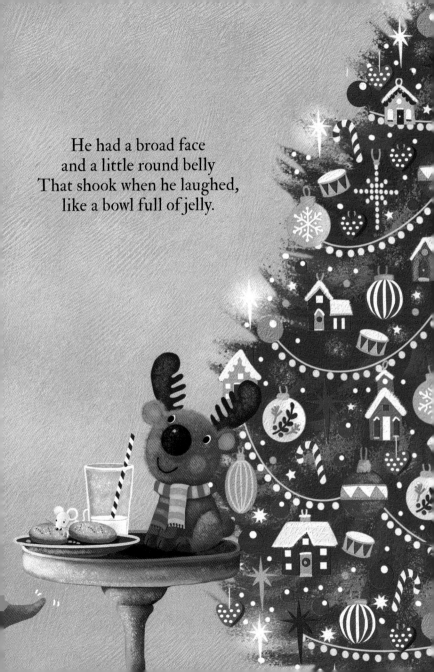

He had a broad face
and a little round belly
That shook when he laughed,
like a bowl full of jelly.

He was chubby and plump,
a right jolly old elf,
And Lily laughed when she saw him,
in spite of herself.

St. Nick winked an eye
and tilted his head
To let Lily know
she had nothing to dread.

He spoke not a word,
but went straight to his work,
Filled Lily's stocking,
then turned with a jerk.

And tapping his finger
at the side of his nose,
And giving a nod,
up the chimney he rose.

He sprang to his sleigh,
to his team gave a whistle,
And away they all flew
like the down of a thistle.
But St. Nicholas exclaimed,
as he drove out of sight—

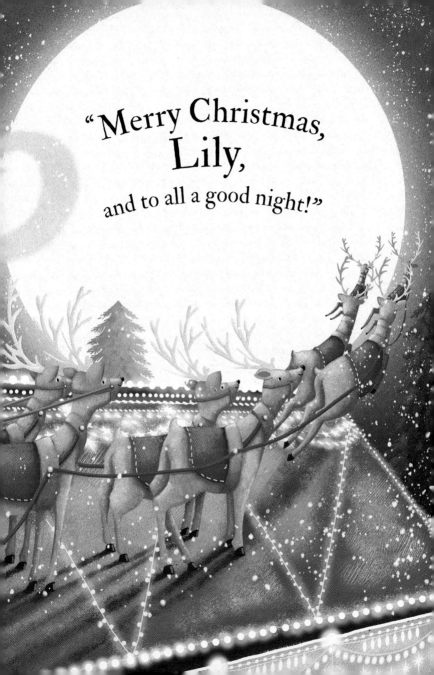

"Merry Christmas,
Lily,
and to all a good night!"

My Christmas Wishes

Lily, can you color in Santa?

To Lily

Adapted from the poem by Clement C. Moore
Illustrated by Jo Parry
Designed by Ryan Dunn and Nicky Scott

Published by Put Me In The Story,
a publication of Sourcebooks.
P.O. Box 4410, Naperville, Illinois 60567-4410
(630) 536-1104
sourcebookskids.com

Date of Production: May 2024
Run Number: 5039043
Printed and Bound in China (GD)
10 9 8 7 6 5 4 3 2 1

MIX
Paper | Supporting
responsible forestry
FSC
www.fsc.org
FSC® C117745

put me
in the story®
Bestselling books starring your child!